CLARA CLAUS
saves
Christmas

CLARA CLAUS
saves
Christmas

Bonnie Bridgman

Illustrated by **Louise Forshaw**

TINY TREE

TINY TREE
CHILDREN'S BOOKS

First Published 2021
Tiny Tree Children's Books
(an imprint of Matthew James Publishing Ltd)
Unit 46, Goyt Mill, Marple, Stockport SK6 7HX

www.tinytreebooks.com

ISBN: 978-1-913230-20-3

To Daisy, Sebby, Ella
and Jaxson - B.B

For Chad, always - L.F

THE FAMIL

CLAUS

Santa's Reindeer

Rudolph
Cheeky. Likes Christmas songs,
especially if they are about him.

Nova
Wonderfully good at directions
and knows every route off by heart.

Dasher
Fastest reindeer (ever).

Comet
Farts. A lot.

Lickety
Short for Lickety-Split. Likes to think he's the fastest
reindeer but is yet to beat Dasher's time.

Halle
Funny.
Brother of Rocket.

Vixen
Best friends with Halle.
Loves to giggle.

Donner
Intuitive – knows immediately what mood Santa is in.
Helps Vespa when Santa needs some encouragement
and works with Halle if Santa needs to Ho! Ho! Ho!

Flea
Strong. Partial to
candy canes.

Prancer
Most handsome reindeer
(according to him).

VESPA

Most relaxed reindeer ever and she's always ready
with a pep talk if Santa ever needs one.

CUPID AND BLITZEN

Twins and mischief-makers. Once ate all of Santa's
cookies because they thought it would be 'funny'. (It
was a bit, but not to Santa.)

MERRI

Actually quite grumpy and not merry at all. Tries to
keep Cupid and Blitzen in check.

DANCER

Doesn't actually like to dance – he prefers sleeping.
Won't move in the morning until he's had his
reindeer-nog.

ROCKET

Halle's Brother. Serious and quiet.
Likes Nova (a lot).

ZIPPY

Known as the Zipster. Chatty. Especially in the
mornings before Dancer has had his reindeer-nog.

COOKIE

Named after Santa's favourite snack. (Cookie's
favourite snack is carrots dunked in Santa's cocoa).

The reindeer were sick.

It started with the wild reindeer. Clara Claus had trundled out into the snow to fetch grasses and leaves so that the reindeer didn't have to go and find food. She'd brought blankets and hay to keep them warm, and she'd made sure there was a fresh supply of water because the lake had frozen over.

Then things got worse – the flying reindeer got sick. And if they couldn't fly, what would happen to Christmas…?

CHAPTER ONE

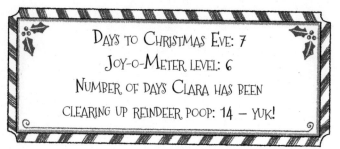
Clara pulled the covers up tighter and crinkled her nose. It was cold in the medical bay of the stables, which was where she'd been sleeping for the past two weeks. She missed her warm cosy bed and the smell of Christmas cookies wafting through the air. But this hard lumpy camp bed would have to do for now. There was no way that Clara would sleep anywhere else. Not when her reindeer were so sick.

As soon as Clara had heard the flying reindeer were ill, she'd rushed to their side to look after them. There she'd stayed, night and day. Clara had cleaned up all their mess (yes, even the stinky brown stuff) and made sure they had enough water and food if they wanted it, which so far they hadn't. Clara was hoping that today – day fourteen of the horrible sickness bug – would be the day the reindeer would eat again. They'd never be strong enough to fly on Christmas Eve if they didn't start chomping on carrots and moss soon.

Clara could hear nearby grunts. Her flying reindeer were awake and ready for attention. She stretched and tossed back the covers, finally dragging herself out of bed and tugging on her warm woolly boots.

No one knew for sure why some reindeer could fly and others couldn't. At the age of two, flying reindeer began to show signs of their special gift, usually with a few leaps that grew steadily higher and higher. But left out in the wild without proper training, these reindeer could hurt themselves (or any nearby snowman!). It was important that Santa, the elves, and most recently Clara stepped in to look after them.

'You can never have too many flying reindeer,' Santa always said, 'or cookies! Ho! Ho! Ho!'

Every year, with more and more children in the world and longer and longer lists, the sleigh had grown heavier. So Santa had added some extra reindeer to the original nine to help pull his sleigh. There were actually eighteen flying reindeer at the North Pole in total. This meant Santa could carry a heavier load, plus it was an even number, so there'd be no more wonky tilts when turning. Extra reindeer also came in handy if one reindeer got sick (although it wasn't helpful when they all did!).

Clara opened the door and Donner's big, dark, sparkling eyes made her heart skip. Donner hadn't looked so alert for weeks.

'Well, good morning, beautiful,' Clara crooned, rushing over to the reindeer. Donner nudged her hand and Clara reached into the red metal bucket on the floor, picked up a carrot and offered it to him, feeling hopeful. Donner scoffed it down in two chomps. Clara chuckled. At least one

reindeer was on the mend. She went to check on the rest and found that nearly all the reindeer were showing signs of feeling better. They were grunting and nuzzling and stomping their hooves for food. All except the twins, Cupid and Blitzen. Both reindeer lay on the straw, groaning. Clara crouched next to them and stroked their heads. She couldn't understand it. All the others were recovering. Dancer had even managed some reindeer-nog (a drink made with milk, cream, and moss) that Clara had made the night before in the hope that it would soon be needed.

She cleared her throat and started to sing 'Jingle Bells', hoping that it would bring comfort to her poorly friends (the reindeer loved a spot of Christmas singing). As Clara sang, Rudolph gave a long growling sound. Although Clara didn't speak reindeer, she knew exactly what Rudolph was saying – 'sing my favourite song'. Unsurprisingly, it was 'Rudolph the Red-Nosed Reindeer', and Rudolph requested it (by snorting and growling until someone sang it) at least three times a day. In fact, Rudolph was so obsessed with the song that last year, he'd 'guided' Santa's sleigh around a little Hampshire village in England four times, making Santa three minutes behind schedule (which is a lot when you have millions of presents to deliver) because he'd heard a choir singing it and hadn't wanted to miss a single note.

Unable to resist making the reindeer happy, Clara opened her mouth to sing Rudolph's song when she noticed something that made her heart sink. Blitzen's tummy was moving up and down quicker than the elves making toys. Fairy lights, what was wrong with them now? Clara peered closer, her heartbeat thudding in her ears. She could barely breathe she was so scared. Then she scowled and jumped to her feet, her hands in fists on her hips.

'Oh, you!' Clara scolded without really meaning it. 'You're not still sick at all!' Cupid and Blitzen were laughing. They'd been tricking her, the rascals! Clara shook her head, then couldn't help but join in with the laughter. The reindeer twins were definitely feeling better if they were back

to their usual pranks. After two long, worrying weeks, Clara felt like ringing sleigh bells with relief. Finally she could enjoy the festive season.

This year was a big year for Clara. She'd been training Nova, and after Rudolph's little mishap last year, Nova would be guiding Santa's sleigh for the first time. Clara felt as proud as a robin that Nova had been selected for this enormous responsibility. This was going to be the best Christmas ever now that the flying reindeer were better.

Little did Clara know, it was only the beginning of her troubles...

CHAPTER TWO

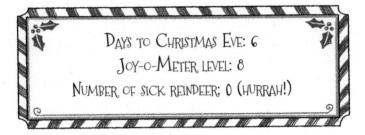

Clara trudged back home from the stables, yawning as the snow squeaked beneath her feet. She pictured herself curled up on the couch, the fire crackling next to her as she watched her favourite Christmas film (Elf). She'd have a bowl of sweet and salty popcorn on her lap and her family by her side. Now that the reindeer were better, Clara would be able to snuggle up in her warm bed (not a cold, lumpy camp bed) and read a book by lamp light. She'd drink a hot chocolate (with mini marshmallows floating on top) that Candy Cane, one of her favourite elves, would make for her. Clara couldn't wait.

Clara Claus, as you've probably realised by now, was the daughter of Santa Claus – or Father Christmas as many preferred to call him. You may know him as Kris Kringle, Pai Natal, Weihnachtsmann, Pére Noël, Papai Noel, Papa Noël or Pops Noel (Clara made that last one up). There were so many different names for Santa that it would probably take from now

until Christmas Day to say them all. Clara knew him best as Dad.

Clara, Santa, her mum (Mrs Claus), and Clara's older brother (Nick) all lived together at the North Pole with the elves and the reindeer, though not in the same house of course. The Claus' home was in the very centre of the North Pole, close to 'all the action', as Santa often said. It was a five-minute walk to the Toy Workshop (Nick had timed it) and four minutes seventeen seconds (thanks, Nick) in the other direction to the flying reindeer stables.

It was a little known fact that Santa didn't live at the North Pole because it was far away from everything or because he loved the cold (although of course he did). It was for a completely different reason. At the edge of the North Pole was a

towering pine tree forest. In the depths of the forest was a cave and at the very centre of the cave magic snow crystals grew. These magic crystals could only be mined by Santa himself and he stored them inside a special Snow Globe. The crystals helped make the sleigh lighter and the reindeer fly higher. And if Santa was ever stuck for an answer, especially with the Naughty and Nice lists, he used the Snow Globe to help make his decision.

Clara smiled when she saw her house in the distance. The outside was made of wood (the colour of milk chocolate) and each window was adorned with red and white gingham curtains. Marzipan flowers were dotted in pretty green window baskets, also made from marzipan (though these often needed replacing thanks to Santa's sweet tooth) and a bird box made of bird seed stood proudly outside the kitchen window. To Clara, home was like a gingerbread house only with less icing but just as enticing. She felt warmer on the inside the closer she got.

Clara swung open her front door. She loved how the smell of freshly baked cookies wafted into her face as soon as she stepped inside, enveloping her in a warm, comforting hug. But today no such smell greeted her. Instead, a strange feeling curled around her shoulders and crept up the back of her neck. The house was as silent as the night. Clara frowned. There were six days until Christmas. It should be chaos central in here – lights ablaze, people rushing to and fro. Not even the fire was lit.

The silence was broken by a noise upstairs. Footsteps. A door shut quietly. Thud, thud, thud. Someone was coming downstairs. Clara widened her eyes at the figure. An elf with white, wiry hair and a green mask covering his mouth. His beady eyes stared out from behind small round glasses.

'What are you doing here?' snapped the man.

Clara stepped back, her reply frozen in her chest. She knew that voice, but who was it?

'Leave now,' he ordered. 'I really must insist.'

'B-b-but it's my house,' squeaked Clara.

The front door slammed and Nick walked in, brushing snow from his hair. 'Clara,' he gasped, 'you're here! I've been looking for you everywhere!' Obviously

not that well, thought Clara, she'd only been at the stables – the same place she'd been for the past fourteen days. 'Dr Elfman,' Nick continued, addressing the masked man, 'do you have a diagnosis?'

That was who it was! Clara hadn't recognised him with the scary mask. Dr Elfman was the only doctor in the North Pole. The rumour was that he never joked, never smiled, and never ate sweets. As far as Clara was concerned, an elf that didn't eat sweets was not to be trusted.

'You both need to leave now,' ordered the doctor.

'Why?' Clara protested.

'I'm afraid Santa Claus is sick,' Doctor Elfman replied.

Clara paled. Santa was sick? Santa was never sick!

'He looked a bit green yesterday after the Santa training,' explained Nick. 'So we called Dr Elfman.'

You might be wondering what Santa training was. Well, Santa was a busy chap and everyone wanted to meet the man himself in the run-up to the big day. There was no way even Santa could be in two million (or more) places at once, especially when he had to sort all the toys, check the lists, and train the reindeer. So Santa had his own personal helpers who were trained to be a Santa but not *the* Santa. These 'Santas' had to be auditioned every year and were carefully monitored to double-check they were suitable candidates. The Santas worked closely with the real Santa, the elves, and the reindeer. So, if you've ever met Santa, chances are it was one of these carefully selected special Santas. Although sometimes the real Santa had been known to pop down to take their place, so it could have been Santa Santa, you'll just never know.

'Well,' continued Dr Elfman, 'Santa's got the same strain of illness that the reindeer had, more than likely. A nasty little stomach virus called Gastro-Tinsel-Itis. Makes the stomach twist, hence the name. Once it's inside your system, it gets absolutely everywhere. Highly contagious. Unfortunately your mother is also showing signs of the virus, which means…you have to stay away.'

'But—' began Clara.

'There are no buts, no exceptions,' the doctor interrupted.

'I just—' Clara tried again.

'Ba, ba, ba, ba,' sung Dr Elfman, waggling his finger in the air at her. Clara wanted to bite it off.

'Christmas Eve is six days away,' Nick pointed out, a look of horror on his face.

'I'm very aware of that, Master Nick. However the facts cannot be changed. The incubation period for Gastro-Tinsel-Itis is at least seven days for humans. Your father exhibited signs twenty-four hours ago which means…' Dr Elfman coughed and adjusted his tie. 'Well, I'm afraid it means that neither your father nor your mother will be recovered until Christmas Day at the earliest.'

Nick and Clara gaped at the doctor.

'Unfortunately,' Dr Elfman went on, 'Binky is also ill. I've quarantined him with Mr and

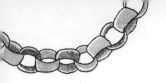

Mrs Claus to prevent the virus spreading any further.'

Clara looked at the doctor and then at Nick. Binky was the head elf. If Santa was out of action, they couldn't do without Binky! This was some sort of joke. It had to be. But no one jumped out at them yelling, 'Gotcha!' Reality slowly sunk into Clara's toes, cementing them to the floor. What were they going to do? Then a thought struck her.

'But I'm not contagious!' she yelled out.

'Quite, my dear,' replied Dr Elfman, taking his glasses off and wiping them with a cloth from his pocket. 'Congratulations.'

'I mean, I spent the most time with the sick reindeer and I'm not ill!'

Dr Elfman peered at Clara over his now spotless glasses. 'Hmm, well, it is entirely plausible that you were the one who infected them both. I would suggest that you are somehow immune to the virus, likely due the amount of time you spend with those creatures. However, any further contact with those infected is not permitted. We could have an outbreak across the North Pole! Your home is now restricted to the patients,' he said, practically shoving the pair out of the door. 'There will be no contact of any kind, including by telephone or email. Is that quite clear? Your parents and Binky need complete rest if they are to make a speedy recovery.' And he slammed the door shut in their faces.

Nick and Clara stared at each other for what felt like the twelve days of Christmas (but was actually only thirty seconds), their mouths opening and shutting like nutcrackers. Dad was sick. Mum was sick. Binky was sick. All of them. Sick. Which meant…figgy pudding! What were they going to do about Christmas?

Clara leant against the front door, banging her head. 'Oh, fairy lights, Christmas is ruined and it's all my fault.'

CHAPTER THREE

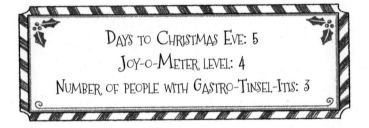

Days to Christmas Eve: 5
Joy-o-Meter level: 4
Number of people with Gastro-Tinsel-Itis: 3

Clara and Nick sat in Dad's office staring into space. Stacks of paper, rows of Christmas cards, and jars of cookies surrounded them. They'd spent a long, silent, and sleepless night in the stables. Not even the reindeer had brought Clara any comfort. What were they going to do?

Santa's office was at the top of the Toy Workshop – an enormous place filled with toys, paper chains and snowflakes. Fairy lights twinkled, music tinkled. Machines whirred

and hammers banged a constant percussion. Fluff and dust flew through the air like an indoor blizzard.

On the workshop floor down below, elves would usually be laughing, singing, and playing with the toys (just to check that they were working of course). But today their joy was replaced with frowns of worry and their singing with muffled murmurs. The elves knew something was wrong – Santa had not been seen all day and now Binky was missing too.

The Joy-o-Meter on the workshop wall was hovering over the number four. Figgy pudding, gulped Clara. It had never been below a five before. The Joy-o-Meter was a device used to measure Christmas Spirit and needed to be on at least three for the magic snow crystals in the Snow Globe to work. The more Christmas Spirit there was, the more powerful the magic. The more powerful the magic, the quicker the toys were made and the higher the reindeer flew. (*Nick vowed that one day he'd find out exactly how it worked, purely for research purposes of course. He was sure it was some sort of chemical reaction.*)

Every year the Joy-o-Meter levels went up and down, but they'd never gone this low before. If Clara and Nick didn't do something soon, it wouldn't matter if Santa got better in time, Christmas would be cancelled.

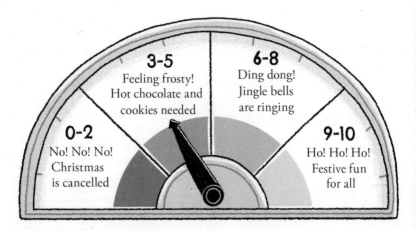

Clara watched as the elves shared looks with each other, some glancing up at Clara in the office. None of them were smiling. You may have a picture of an elf in your mind: pointy hat, rosy cheeks, bells on shoes, that sort of thing. And although Santa's elves loved a good shoe bell, they were hardly appropriate workshop footwear. I mean, imagine dropping a hammer with only a bell to protect your toes. Toy making required steel-capped boots, green overalls, red and white checked T-shirts, and strictly no pom-poms – a pom-pom on a hat was a serious health and safety issue if it obscured your vision whilst operating heavy machinery.

Elves came in all different shapes and sizes – not all were little. In fact, elves looked just like you, or the person next to you (or your next door neighbour or your next door neighbour's neighbour's neighbour). The only differences between elves and humans were that elves wore a lot more sparkly things, they loved anything jingly, and their favourite colour was always green. They were also happier than humans, who for some reason, seemed to see the worst in things. Elves always looked on the bright side. Until today.

Clara raised her hand and waved at Candy Cane on the workshop floor below. Candy didn't wave back, but frowned.

Oh, Christmas crackers! Clara thought. That wasn't good. Candy always had a smile for Clara. How in Kris Kringle were they going to save Christmas? The worried elves were working more slowly than usual, which meant that toy production was already behind, especially with Binky, the head elf, ill. And with Santa sick, there was no one to deliver the presents. The lower the Joy-o-Meter got, the less magic there was and there wouldn't be enough to keep the reindeer flying for the whole of Christmas Eve. If it went below three… Christmas stockings…that would be a disaster!

Clara's heartbeat raced as she thought of the billions of children around the world who

would be disappointed on Christmas morning. She felt the room begin to spin and grabbed hold of the desk in front of her. Clara took deep breaths, steadying herself, and saw a small figure moving towards them, her red hair gleaming like a beacon. Jingle bells! Clara felt a surge of hope. It was Cocoa, Binky's equally efficient daughter. She would know what to do.

Cocoa clanged her way up the black metal steps to the office, a clipboard clutched to her chest. The elves below in the workshop watched on closely.

'Smile,' hissed Cocoa as she approached, then whispered, 'So, what's the plan?'

Plan? What plan? Clara fretted. Clara's plan had been that Cocoa would have a plan. There was no other plan.

'Well,' Nick announced with a click of his pen, placing it proudly on the paper before him. 'I've written a list.'

'Did you check it twice?' Clara quipped. She always joked when she was nervous. Nick and Cocoa glared at her, unsmiling. Clara sighed and pulled the list towards her.

Christmas to-do list by Nick Claus Junior, to be completed by <u>Christmas Eve</u>

'Um? To be completed by Christmas Eve?' Clara asked. Surely that was obvious.

'Just making it clear,' Nick replied. (*It never hurt to be clear, Nick thought.*)

'O-kay.' Clara nodded slowly, and continued reading.

Job one: Get the elves working at full speed

The elves were already working slower than they should be. The news that Santa was sick and probably wouldn't fly on Christmas Eve was going to be bad enough. Then there was the fact that Binky, head elf, friend, and colleague, was also sick and that two inexperienced children who argued all the time were in charge of the Christmas rescue mission. They had to get the elves to trust them, and fast.

'I might have an idea about job two,' Nick said, beaming.

'Of course you do,' Clara retorted. She wasn't surprised. Lists were Nick's area of expertise and Santa's lists were particularly complicated. Santa had to liaise with lots of different people for every child's Christmas list. And every household did Christmas differently. In some houses, the parents bought one present and Santa brings another. In other houses, it was just Santa's gifts that a child would receive. Some presents had to be delivered for Christmas Eve (morning), ready to be opened on Christmas Eve (evening) and other presents needed to be delivered in time to be opened on Christmas Day. These variations were mostly down to traditions and also because Santa and his team had not always been quite as efficient as they were today.

Santa always tried to make everyone's Christmas special, but didn't always bring the present requested. Sometimes he felt pyjamas were a better gift than roller skates, or he spotted the perfect book instead. It didn't mean that a child hadn't been good, it just meant he thought a little differently. And, after all, it was the thought that counted, right?

'Efficiency-wise,' Cocoa said before Nick could explain his idea, 'it would be beneficial

to administer each job to the most suitable candidate, which would be impossible to do without knowing what all those jobs were. Therefore, I would recommend completing the reading of the jobs list in order for us to make the appropriate delegation.'

Nick pursed his lips and nodded. Clara didn't have a clue what Cocoa had just said so she just nodded too and carried on reading the list.

Job Three: Reindeer

'What's the matter with the reindeer?' Clara asked, her heart pounding in her chest. She felt sick at the thought that another bout of Gastro-Tinsel-Itis had struck.

'We're two weeks behind schedule with the training,' Nick explained. 'Plus the reindeer are not at their full strength after their sickness.'

Clara breathed out. Thank stockings for that! She'd been terrified that something else had happened to them. Training she could handle. Hold on… 'Training?' Her face practically lit up like Rudolph's nose.

Before Clara could say any more, Cocoa pointed to the next item on the list.

Job Four: Check Naughty and Nice lists (twice)
up until Christmas Eve (mid-morning)

That's right, every child had until Christmas Eve to make it onto the Nice list. And, as Clara had witnessed herself, there was nothing like a last-minute change to get the adrenaline pumping.

Job Five: Confer with Santa Scouts

Santa Scouts made job four a fair bit easier for Santa. Scouts were those gorgeously cute red-breasted robins that flew everywhere, especially at Christmas time. Although sometimes Santa used different birds if the climate of the country you were from did not have robins. Parrots, hornbills, and even chickens had been used as

Santa Scouts, to varying degrees of success –
chickens were not the best at remembering.

Santa Scouts chatted to the worms in your
garden and the spiders in your home. They
found out if you'd been naughty, and they
knew if you'd been good. They saw everything.
So there you have it – Santa had eyes and ears
everywhere. Beware and be good!

Job Six: Deliver the presents to all the children on
the Nice list and have a very merry Christmas!

And relax, thought Clara.

CHAPTER FOUR

DAYS TO CHRISTMAS EVE: 5
JOY-O-METER LEVEL: 4
CHRISTMAS TO-DO LISTS: 1 – THANKS, NICK!

'Many of the jobs require precision and efficiency, particularly the list-based tasks,' began Cocoa.

Nick nodded. 'I agree. We've already lost precious time and we can't afford to lose any more. Statistics show that when productivity...'

Clara watched as Nick and Cocoa droned on. She could think of nothing worse than lists, statistics, and efficiency. The reindeer, however – now that was a job for her. Oh, what

fun it would be to ride on a sleigh, practising the routes. Maybe she'd even get to be the one delivering the presents on Christmas Eve! Nick wasn't exactly a reindeer person, or even a people person. He was a list person. Where as I, thought Clara, I could holler out a 'Ho! Ho! Ho!' whilst Nova soared high and...

Clara felt prickles on her skin and crashed down to reality. Someone was watching her. Two someones in fact – Nick and Cocoa were both staring and frowning. Oops. Had they been talking to her? Clara grinned at them sheepishly.

Nick sighed. 'Clara, have you been paying any attention? We've got a job to do, you know.' He looked across at Cocoa as if to say, Look what I've got to put up with.

Nick didn't think she could do anything right, thought Clara. He was always so serious. Of course, saving Christmas was serious, but Nick always made things so…not fun.

Clara pulled her shoulders back and held her head high. 'We should probably do job one together,' she said, 'to show we're a team.' Clara wished Nick would remember they were on the same team, but bit her tongue to stop herself from adding that. (*In actual fact, Nick was thinking the same thing. He wished that Clara would take something seriously for once.*) Clara continued, 'Without the elves on our side, there'll be no toys. And with no toys, the Joy-o-Meter will drop even further and then… Christmas will definitely be cancelled!'

The others agreed. It was time to tell the elves.

Clara and Nick heaved themselves up from the safety of their chairs in Santa's office. Before they headed out onto the balcony above the workshop floor, Nick grabbed Clara's arm and announced with wide eyes, 'I've got an idea.'

'Nick, I don't think now's the—'

Clara was cut off, rather rudely, by Cocoa. 'Tick-tick-tock.' The elf tapped her watch repeatedly.

Nick dashed off into Santa's toilet and emerged in what Clara could only describe as the worst plan ever. He was dressed as Dad. Kind of. The Santa suit was enormous on Nick.

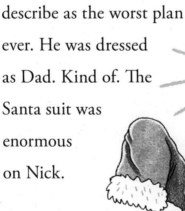

'Give me your coat, Clara, so I can pad this out.' Nick gestured to his belly.

Clara frowned. 'Nick, I really don't think—' she began.

'Listen, if I look like Dad, then it will reassure the elves that I can be Dad.'

Clara shook her head. Just because you looked like Santa didn't mean you were Santa, especially if you were a twelve-year-old boy. Everyone knew that. But Cocoa simply shrugged her shoulders and opened the door for Nick.

'Don't mess it up,' Cocoa hissed unhelpfully from behind them, still clutching her clipboard. 'We haven't got the time.'

'Useful advice,' muttered Clara under her breath.

'Shhh!' snapped Nick. 'Everyone is watching us.' Nick cleared his throat. 'Um... Ho! Ho!

Ho!' he hollered in what Clara assumed was his best Santa impression. (She thought it was terrible.) The elves stopped and stared. Clara didn't blame them.

'Um, hi. I'm Nick,' he began, addressing the elves below.

'I think they know who you are, Nick,' quipped Clara, but just in case they didn't, she added, 'And I'm Clara.' She waved and gave a sort of half laugh, half snort, which sounded a bit like a reindeer farting.

Clara could feel sweat building on her top lip. How in all of the North Pole were they going to achieve anything from their list when they couldn't even do job one? Beside her, Nick was still and silent. His face had the look of a melting snowman. Cocoa looked at her watch then at Clara with her eyebrows raised.

'Okay,' Clara started, 'we've got a bit of bad news. Dad is sick and most likely won't be better by Christmas.' Clara paused as loud murmurs rippled through the elf crowd. 'Unfortunately, Mum and Binky are ill too,' she added. The

noise grew and the elves were now scowling. Clara glanced over at the Joy-o-Meter. It was hovering over number three! *Figgy pudding!* Clara thought. She had to fix this and fast. 'We need your help. We need you to get back to work. Nick and I are going to sort everything out, don't worry…'

Cocoa coughed and raised her eyebrows at Clara.

'And Cocoa too,' Clara added hurriedly. 'We're all working together and have everything under control. So please, go back to work just as before.'

Cocoa ahemed again and clicked her pen on her clipboard.

'Well, okay, a little quicker than before,' Clara said, laughing nervously. 'We've got some numbers to make up. Look, it's going to be hard and messy and there may be some shouting and—'

'Lists!' interrupted Nick.

Clara chuckled. 'Yes, oodles of lists! But together we can do this. Together we can save Christmas!'

Clara punched her hand in the air for extra impact. If she was honest, she expected some sort of cheering or loud clapping. But there was nothing.

Awkward.

Then Mistletoe, one of the senior elves, nodded and went back to work. One by one, the other elves in the workshop followed. Within two minutes, the workshop was a hub of activity again, including 'Dominic the Donkey' (a firm elf favourite) booming out from ELF FM. The elves sang along and Clara watched as the Joy-o-Meter etched its way back up to five. Phew.

Clara let out the longest sigh of relief and saw the colour trickle back into her brother's cheeks. She smiled at him. They'd done it. They'd got the elves to go back to work. *Oh, my Christmas crackers*, Clara thought, *we've saved*—

'That's job one done. On to job two!' announced Cocoa as she consulted her clipboard and crossed job one off Nick's list.

Right, job two… there was still a long way to go.

CHAPTER FIVE

DAYS TO CHRISTMAS EVE: 4
JOY-O-METER LEVEL: 5
NUMBER OF FLYING REINDEER TO TRAIN:
18 – CLARA COULDN'T WAIT!

Clara dashed across the lamplit path, past her house, and over to the stables. She couldn't wait to start reindeer training. She'd left Nick and Cocoa (and her clipboard) in charge of job two – checking the toys and co-ordinating the lists. They'd all agreed that Clara was the best person for job three. Obviously.

Half of the reindeer were prancing in the snow as she neared. She put her fingers in her mouth and blew, sending a piercing whistle through the air. The reindeer pricked up their ears and Nova came galloping over to Clara, nudging at her hand with her snout. Clara took off her glove so that she could stroke Nova properly and scratch that bit behind the antlers that Nova loved so much. They were soon joined by most of the other flying reindeer. Clara knew that Prancer would be the last to join them – he always liked to make an entrance so that all eyes were looking at him.

Clara adored everything about her reindeer. The feel of their fur. How their eyes changed colour depending on the season – in the summer they were a beautiful golden shade and a cool and frosty blue in the winter. She loved their different personalities and the fact they were always as happy to see her as she was to see them, even Rudolph, who was still a little mad at her for training Nova so well.

'Okay, we are two weeks behind schedule and we need to get you back to peak fitness,' Clara began.

Lickety snorted, steam bellowing out of his nostrils as he stomped his hoof.

'You might be fast, Lickety, but not as fast as you were before you got sick. We've got a lot of work to do! Unfortunately Santa has the same bug you had, but…'

Cookie whimpered next to her and Clara walked over to soothe the reindeer.

'Don't worry,' Clara continued. 'I'm going to make sure you're the best you've ever been.'

Clara started by organising short races and sprints to give the reindeer some exercise. The route went up to and around Clara's house and back to the stables again before flying upwards to trace the same route in the air. Clara hoped that Mum and Dad were watching from their bedroom window so they knew that everything was all right (and Clara really hoped it would be, for Christmas' sake). She made sure that Lickety and Dasher weren't in the same group (Lickety would wear himself out trying to beat the fastest reindeer), then whistled for the reindeer to start.

'Hi, Clara,' a voice said beside her once the reindeer were off. She turned to see Jingles, an elf around Nick's age with charcoal hair and chestnut eyes. Jingles preferred working in the stables to the Toy Workshop and knew almost as much about reindeer as Clara did.

'Are they all eating properly now?' Clara asked the elf.

Jingles nodded. 'Yes, and I'm giving them as much reindeer-nog as they want. Although apparently I don't make it as well as you do.' Jingles rolled his eyes.

Clara smiled and continued to listen to Jingles' report whilst watching the reindeer. Her smile dropped. There was something wrong. Where were Cupid and Blitzen?

Clara whistled to bring the reindeer back from their races. 'Where are the others?' Clara demanded. They all shook their heads, panting from their exercise.

'Continue practising,' Clara said to the reindeer. 'Nova, you're in charge.' Rudolph snorted and Clara sighed. 'Fine, Nova, you take Comet,

Cookie, Prancer, Halle, Rocket, Vixen, and…'
Clara was getting muddled, already forgetting
which reindeer she'd put in Nova's group. 'Zippy.
Everyone else, you're with Rudolph, okay?
Practise the route around the North Pole and
see if you can beat each other's times. Jingles
and I are going to see if we can find Cupid and
Blitzen.' Clara looked at Jingles, who nodded
back. 'Just…keep training, okay?'

'The twins seemed fine earlier,' Jingles puffed
as he and Clara dashed off. It was getting dark
now and the temperature at the North Pole
was dropping fast.

'Oh, I'm sure they are,' Clara replied. 'But we
don't have enough time for their mischief. Not
with so much training to catch up on!'

Jingles' eyes widened. 'You don't think they'd…'

'Oh, I'm sure they would,' answered Clara. She was certain the reindeer twins were up to their usual tricks.

'Follow me,' Clara said, gesturing to Jingles as they got closer to the stables. She held up a finger to her lips.

They tiptoed towards the building, ducking underneath the windows so the reindeer couldn't see them approach. Clara slowly pulled open the door. A gust of snow swirled its way into the room. She heard the clattering of hooves on the stone floor.

'I know you're in here!' Clara called.

Silence.

'Are you sure...?' whispered Jingles.

Clara raised her eyebrows and waited. There it was! Snorting, growing louder and louder. Clara rolled her eyes at the reindeer's guffaws.

Splat! A snowball pelted her on the arm. Clara stood open-mouthed. Big mistake. It was an irresistible target for Cupid. Using his hoof to nudge a snowball (which he'd hidden inside a feed bucket) onto his nose he aimed and…fired! *Whoosh! Thwack! Splat!* Ice cold snow smacked Clara in the face. Bits of snowball dripped off her nose and chin. Jingles gasped next to her, pushing his hand against his mouth to stifle his laughter. Clara shook her head, wiped away the rest of the snow,

and stomped towards the reindeer. 'It's not funny, you two!'

The sniggering snorts coming from Cupid and Blitzen said that they disagreed with her.

'Santa's sick, you know.'

The reindeer stopped laughing and peeped out from their hiding place, their antlers covered in straw.

'So are Mum and Binky. We've got a lot to do to get everything ready for Christmas and…' The realisation of the enormity of what she had to do washed over Clara, weighing her down. She panted, taking short breath after short breath, over and over again. She could feel Jingles's hand on her arm, but that didn't help. What if they couldn't do it? What if they couldn't save Christmas? What if the reindeer weren't trained on time? What if the sleigh was too heavy to fly? What if Santa didn't get better by Christmas Eve? Who would deliver the presents? What if—

Clara felt a warm, rough tongue lick her cheek, interrupting her worries. Then another came on the opposite side. She looked from one concerned reindeer face to the other, took a deep breath and sighed. 'Thank you,' she whispered to her reindeer.

As she buried her face into Blitzen's neck, Clara took a deep breath. *I can do this*, she said to herself. 'Little drops make big rivers.' Clara's mum always said that when Nick and Clara were disappointed for only baking one tray of cookies compared to Mum's eight. 'It all adds up,' Mrs Claus would clarify. Mum was right. All Clara needed to do was focus on her job of training the reindeer, then she could move on to the next task. Before she knew it, Christmas would be saved.

Clara thought about that a lot that night whilst she was lying in her cold lumpy camp bed, listening to her brother mumble about lists and efficiency in his sleep. She would be the best reindeer trainer ever, although she'd have to split up Cupid and Blitzen first. Now they knew how important it was not to pull any more pranks, she was sure that they wouldn't. But Clara wasn't going to take any chances, not with Christmas at stake.

CHAPTER SIX

Days to Christmas Eve: 3
Joy-o-Meter level: 7
Number of hours Clara slept last night
thanks to Nick's nattering: 3

Jingles had taken Rudolph's reindeer group to run races across the snow whilst Clara worked with Nova's.

Everything was running smoothly, although Comet was farting more than usual and the smell was burning Clara's nose.

'Come on, Cookie!' Clara called to the reindeer. She clicked her stopwatch as the reindeer crossed the finish line – a row of carrots in the snow. Clara checked her list (she felt like Nick) and spotted a problem. When she hadn't been thinking straight yesterday, she'd put Dasher and Lickety-Split in Rudolph's group together. She hoped Jingles could handle them. Lickety was great on his own, but when Dasher was around, all he could think about was beating her time.

'Clara!' called a voice. Clara looked up from her clipboard (figgy pudding, was she turning into Cocoa too?) and saw the clipboard-loving elf glaring as she stomped over to her. Then Clara saw something else. A blizzard of swirling snow. And it was barrelling straight towards them! Clara strained her eyes trying to get a closer look. Deck the halls! It was Dasher, followed closely (but not too closely) by Lickety. They were racing!

'Out of the way!' Clara shouted to the elf, who seemed to be frozen to the ground. Cocoa stared at Dasher and Lickety, her eyes wide. 'Move!' she tried again, but Cocoa still wouldn't budge.

Clara had no choice. She propelled herself through the air, grabbing Cocoa and knocking her to the ground. Snow covered Clara's ears, jamming down her back. She heaved herself up. 'Are you all right?' Clara asked the elf who had yet to say a word.

'Am I all right?' Cocoa gritted her teeth. 'I see you're about as efficient as your brother!' *Uh oh!* Clara nibbled her bottom lip. *What had Nick done now?*

🍬 🍬 🍬

Nick hadn't done anything. That was the problem.

'He's been stuck in your father's office for the most part of the morning and indeed yesterday,'

Cocoa told Clara as they hurried over to the Toy Workshop. Clara had given Lickety a stern word and put Jingles in charge before she'd left the reindeer. 'The elves are still working at a satisfactory level of speed, which is unsurprising as elves are magnificent, but this amount of ineptitude is unacceptable and further more…'

'Cocoa!' Clara interrupted. 'I don't understand what you're saying!'

Cocoa inhaled sharply and blinked. They were at the workshop now anyway, so Clara could just find out for herself. She yanked open the door and was greeted by the sound of elves singing 'We Need a Little Christmas', Nick's favourite song. The scent of cinnamon filled the air – Mistletoe must have made his delicious pastries again.

It looked as if they'd arrived at the right time because Nick was standing halfway up the staircase ready to address the elves below.

'I've had an exceptional idea,' Nick announced in an annoying superior-sounding voice. 'A plan to revolutionise the toy-making process. I have developed a Toy Popularity Prediction Algorithm or, as I call it, a T.P.P.A.' Nick gestured to a huge thing next to him covered in a red and white gingham sheet. Clara gulped. No good sentence started with 'I've developed a Toy Popularity Prediction Algorithm'.

It seemed that Clara wasn't the only person to have doubts about Nick's plan. Ginger, a tall elf with plaits curled into buns each side of her head, was leaning against a counter, legs crossed in front of her. Meanwhile, Candy was glaring at Nick, and Clara was pretty sure that Twinkle-Toes, an elderly elf, had gone to sleep. Nick continued, oblivious to the growing hostility.

'My algorithm monitors past toy trends in combination with the current toy lists received. By inputting all the data into my equation, we are able to predict future trends.'

'Fascinating,' said Cocoa, walking slowly through the workshop towards Nick. 'So you utilise a computer to calculate which products we need to increase in production?'

'Well…' Nick rubbed the back of his neck. 'Not exactly. I tried that, but I couldn't get it to work so…' Nick pulled down the gingham sheet. 'Ta da!'

'Cool! A spinning thingy,' said Clara, taking in the bright yellow machine about the size of Nick with a huge round wheel on the front and a spinning arrow attached. The wheel was divided into sections, each a different colour.

'Well, it's a highly sophisticated piece of equipment powered by Snow Globe magic using the data we've collected over past years and...'

As Nick talked, Clara watched him spin the wheel. It made a really satisfying clackety-clack sound before dinging when it stopped on a toy. In this instance the section was showing building blocks.

'And now we know we need to make more building blocks!' Nick paused and looked around the room, beaming.

Cocoa was riveted. No one else was. All elf eyebrows were furrowed in the middle.

Nick tried again. 'It means we can always be prepared. There'll be no more making toys at the last minute or panicking because we have run out of a particular part. We would have already made the required toys in advance!'

'So you've made a crystal ball?' Candy said, her eyebrows raised, unimpressed.

'What was wrong with the way we made toys before?' asked Ginger.

Clara bit her lip. The elves were getting cross. She glanced at the Joy-o-Meter and saw it was dropping down to five.

Nick cleared his throat. 'Well, nothing, but it wasn't very efficient so—'

'Oh, so we're inefficient elves, are we?' Candy interrupted. 'What could we possibly know about toy-making after having done it for hundreds of years? No more than a twelve-year-old boy with a spinning wheel, that's for sure.'

'You don't understand… it's… it's not a-a spinning wheel… I'm not… What I mean is,' Nick pressed on, 'I've built a programme which allows us to monitor…' Nick looked deflated, like a balloon that had been popped. Clara felt her heart sink for him.

'You said it helps us to monitor. Who is us?' asked Mistletoe.

'Well…' Nick shook his head and raised his shoulders. 'Anyone one who's looking at it.'

'Oh, anyone. So anyone can make toys now?' Candy said. 'Why bother having us elves at all!'

'No, no, no, no, that's not what I'm saying,' protested Nick.

'Sounded like what you were saying,' Twinkle-Toes said.

'No, I wasn't!'

'Don't yell at us! Santa never yells at us,' Candy pointed out.

'Please, just calm down—' Nick said.

'Calm down?' Candy thwacked her hand on the table, flinging a ruler high into the air. 'I'll show you calm down, Nicholas Claus!' Candy stomped to the front so she was facing the workshop elves. 'It seems like us elves aren't good enough for Mr Algorithm.'

The elves murmured and nodded.

'I say we strike!' yelled Candy.

The elves cheered.

'I say we march!' They whooped.

'I say we show Mr Algorithm just what us elves are made of!'

Placards suddenly appeared displaying protests including 'Yule be sorry!' 'Sleigh what?' and Clara's personal favourite, 'Believe in your elf!' (Clara wondered where they had come from. Did the elves always have them in case strike action was needed?)

The elves began marching in circles across the workshop floor with chants filling the air.

'Elf appreciation!'

'You're not Santa!'

'Ick to Nick!'

The noise was deafening – louder than all

the toy machines put together. Nick was getting more and more flustered, his face now as red as Santa's hat. Cocoa was frantically trying to talk to the other elves, but no one was listening.

A rather big and burly elf named Baubles had started to whack the spinning wheel with his placard.

Clara couldn't watch any more. The Joy-o-Meter had dropped to three! Not knowing what else to do, Clara used one of her reindeer training techniques. She put her fingers in her mouth and blew, sending a piercing whistle across the room.

The elves hushed and all eyes shot to Clara Claus.

She held her hands up in the air. 'I think there's been a…misunderstanding or a miss… explained… thing.' Clara glared at Nick. 'Look… Nick, you're great with lists – really brilliant at them, the best actually and… I'm sure you're good at other things…' Clara was certain he was good at something else, she just couldn't think of anything right then. 'But you are not good with people. At all.'

The elves nodded and Clara turned back to them. 'Every year, you elves work really hard, and every year there's a last-minute rush to make a particular toy that no one knew was going to be so popular. Right?' Clara took the elves' mumbles as a good sign. 'Every year you work

harder and faster, just so you
can make all children's
dreams come true.
You're miracle
workers really. Nick
is trying to help us
prepare. If we use his
Christmas spinner—'

'Algorithm!' Nick butted in.

'Whatever,' replied Clara, making a face (she
knew exactly what it was called, but it was
much more fun annoying Nick). 'If we use the
Christmas spinner, we can predict what's going
to be popular and make sure we have enough
of it. That's right, isn't it, Nick?'

Nick nodded slowly and looked around
the room.

'Of course, we wouldn't be able to do any of this without your elf-pertise,' Clara went on, sensing that the elf tempers were simmering down. 'We know this is going to be tough without Santa, and we cannot do it without you.'

Clara nibbled her bottom lip. Like before, there was no reaction to Clara's speech. But to her relief, the placards vanished as quickly as they had appeared and the Joy-o-Meter was nudging up to four. Clara scarpered before anything else went wrong.

CHAPTER SEVEN

After preventing an elf riot (single-handedly, thank you very much) and surviving charging reindeer, Clara felt she and Jingles deserved some hot chocolate. She trundled off to the kitchens and walked back to the stables carefully carrying the steaming hot drinks (with oodles of extra marshmallows for her and extra whipped cream for Jingles). Now that the toys were sorted, Nick had moved on to the Naughty and Nice lists whilst Cocoa was conferring with the Santa

Scouts. Clara whistled a little 'We Wish You a Merry Christmas,' pleased that they'd managed to get the first two jobs done.

After she'd drunk every last dribble of her hot chocolate whilst the reindeer were on a break, Clara focused on the next job that was bothering her – flying the sleigh. Although she'd spent a lot

of time with the reindeer, Clara had never flown the sleigh before. She sat down in the driver's seat and looked at all the buttons in front of her (and there were a lot of buttons) and then at the manual that Jingles had given her before disappearing with a flimsy excuse about washing up the hot chocolate mugs.

The manual was huge. Enormous. She'd never seen a book so big before. Not even The Ultimate Christmas Carol Songbook was this long. She

dropped the manual on the snow with a thud and decided to look at the buttons instead. Surely there must be some kind of 'on' switch. There wasn't. There wasn't even a key.

Clara growled and stomped out of the sleigh to pick up the manual. 'Ho! Ho! Ho!' the first line read. 'Ho! Ho! Ho!' she repeated in a grumble.

To her shock, and utter delight, lights suddenly twinkled on the front and the dashboard lit up. The sleigh was on!

Until the lists were complete, Clara didn't know how heavy the sleigh was going to be on Christmas Eve. It would be lighter than it should be thanks to the Snow Globe magic, but it would still be pretty heavy for the reindeer. They needed to practise flying whilst pulling some kind of weight. Clara didn't know how they usually prepared, but she decided that adding carrots and hay from the stables to the sleigh would give the reindeer some sort of load to carry.

With Rudolph and his group training with Jingles, Clara practised riding the sleigh with hers. She attached the deep red reins onto the reindeer and fastened the glistening gold buckles to secure each reindeer in place. Taking a deep breath, Clara clipped the reins to the sleigh and tugged to make sure she'd done it right. Fairy lights, she thought with a gulp, I can't believe I'm about to ride the sleigh! She took her seat, feeling joy wash over her.

'Ho! Ho! Ho! And away we go!' hollered Clara, reading the next page of the manual. The ground juddered beneath the sleigh and Clara felt herself lifting up in the air. *Jingle bells!* she thought as she clicked her sleigh belt into place. *This is incredible!* At the front, Nova soared through the air along the route she'd been following in training. Despite the cold, Clara felt her insides warm up as her hair streamed in the wind and she glanced down at the snowy North Pole below. She saw the snow-covered treetops of the forest and the frozen lake glistening in the sun. Snowmen stood proudly like children below and Clara couldn't resist waving to them. The reindeer were magnificent, galloping along in time with each other. Zipster was chattering away and beaming, clearly as delighted as Clara was. Riding in the sleigh truly was every bit as magical as Clara had dreamt it would be.

It was time for Nova to turn. The sleigh whipped around, sending Clara squishing over to one side, but safe under her sleigh belt. Uh oh, thought Clara. What were those vibrations below her bottom and feet? Something was rolling. A lot of somethings. In her haste to start practising, Clara had left the carrots loose. And of course, they didn't have sleigh belts! Carrots began flying out of the sleigh, dropping to the ground like snowballs – only harder, pointier, and a lot more orange.

'Look out!' Clara yelled as elves travelling to the workshop ran for cover. She flicked to next page of the manual. 'No! No! No!' she read aloud. 'Return to the stables!' Carrots continued to fly through the air like carrot-sleet. The hay joined in now too, covering Clara completely

※ 93 ※

until she resembled a straw snowman. All she needed was one of the flying carrots for her nose. At last they landed with a gentle bump and Clara sighed. She brushed off the straw and jumped out to soothe the reindeer who were a little shaken up by the carrot and hay tornado Clara had caused. She felt sorry for poor Nova as Rudolph and his group looked on, snorting, Nova held her head high despite the other reindeers' chortles. *And so she should*, thought Clara. The carrot fiasco had been her fault, not Nova's. Clara nibbled her bottom lip. *Well, at least she'd know not to do that again!*

🍬 🍬 🍬

Clara's back ached as she woke the next morning. She stretched up high as if putting the star on top of a Christmas tree. *Ah, that felt good.* Nick had spent the night in Dad's office and Clara had slept quite well without his sleep nattering.

A rat-a-tat-tat on the door made her jump. Jingles stepped inside, frowning as he rushed towards her.

'We've got a problem,' he said.

'What's wrong?' Clara was confused. It was barely six o'clock in the morning. How could there possibly be a problem already?

'Come with me,' Jingles said, his jaw clenched. 'It's better if you see for yourself.'

Clara felt sick as she followed Jingles to the workshop in her pyjamas. As soon as she stepped inside the room, she knew something was wrong. There was no whirring or churning, no banging or bashing. It was early, but the elves had usually started by now. They needed much less sleep than humans. Clara's eyes shot to Jingles.

'The machines are broken. We've tried fixing them but… There's nothing technically wrong with them. It's…'

Jingles pointed at the Joy-o-Meter on the wall. The arrow was down at zero.

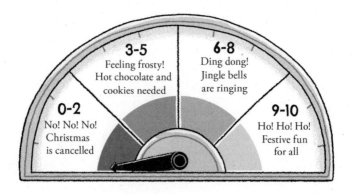

CHAPTER EIGHT

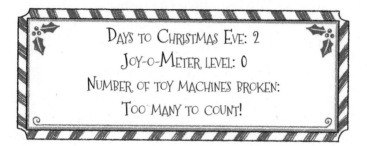

DAYS TO CHRISTMAS EVE: 2
JOY-O-METER LEVEL: 0
NUMBER OF TOY MACHINES BROKEN:
TOO MANY TO COUNT!

One problem at a time, thought Clara. *Little drops make big rivers.* 'Can we make the toys by hand?' she asked hopefully.

'Some of them,' answered Jingles, 'but some toys need the machines. Plus if we make everything by hand, we definitely won't meet the quota we need.'

'So not every child will get a gift,' Clara sighed, hope draining out of her.

Jingles shook his head. 'Not even with all the books and toys and games we have in reserve.'

Clara puffed out her cheeks. It didn't matter anyway. With the Joy-o-Meter on zero, there'd be no Christmas Spirit to make the sleigh light enough to fly and the… Oh, my fairy lights! Clara raced out of the workshop. The reindeer!

As Clara neared the stables, she saw Nova. She watched as her darling, sweet reindeer galloped across the snow and leapt high into the air. Clara held her breath and silently screamed as Nova thudded to the ground, bouncing and skidding along the floor.

'Nova!' Clara cried, rushing over to her. The reindeer dragged herself back up and Clara nestled her head on Nova's neck. 'This can't be happening,' Clara whimpered. She nuzzled

Nova for a while, patting her gently, until finally opening her eyes.

Jingles was standing in front of them, his face pale and hopeless.

'I don't know what to do,' Clara admitted.

Jingles smiled sadly at her. 'I don't know what you can do.'

Clara shook her head. This can't be it, she thought. We can't have failed. There must be some way to fix it...

'Nick!' Clara said. 'He'll know what to do! He's bound to have a list or an algorithm for this kind of thing.'

Clara and Jingles raced back across to the workshop and barged into Santa's office without so much as a knock. The sight that greeted them was not what they were expecting.

Completing the Naughty and Nice lists was a complicated affair. No child was simply naughty or nice – it would be much easier if they were. There wasn't a points-based system that said ten good deeds gave you fifty points and two hundred points got you on the Nice list, bam! Nor was there a system of three strikes and you were out, straight onto the Naughty list. Nope, Santa's Scouts were watching all year long. They wanted the children to be the best they could be and they never compared anyone to anybody else (what would be the point?). For example, a child may not have been able to help around her house because she'd broken her arm. Should she be on the Naughty list for that? Not on your nutcrackers! Equally, a child may have been helping his parent but only to get the treat he'd been promised. Should that mean he would be on the Nice list? Hmm, debatable…

Santa Scouts were there to check that each child was trying, that they were kind, and that they did their best. The information collected by the Santa Scouts was use to help place children into different categories, with the choices subject to change right until the last minute on Christmas Eve:

Naughty

Nice

Nearly Naughty

Nearly Nice

Undecided (which was usually the biggest box)

This however didn't not compute with what Clara and Jingles saw lying in the centre of the office – just three labels:

The Nice box was full, the Naughty box was overflowing (there were actually seventeen Naughty boxes), and the Undecided box was…

empty. There were no other boxes and no other names left to be sorted.

Cocoa and Nick looked at Clara and Jingles from Santa's desk and smiled smugly as they sipped on mugs of hot chocolate.

'We've finished!' Nick beamed proudly.

Clara was stunned. *How could they possibly be finished?*

Nick smiled, obviously pleased with himself and oblivious to how much Clara wanted to wallop him.

'Surprised, Clara Claus?' cooed Cocoa. 'I finished with the Santa Scouts early and so came to assist Nick here.'

Clara balled her hands into fists and took a deep breath. 'Why is the Undecided box empty?' she asked, glancing from Nick to Cocoa.

Nick grinned. (*He'd known Clara would be surprised*.) 'Because there are no Undecideds. We finished the lists.'

Clara couldn't speak, not without exploding. Who would do such a silly, idiotic, moronic thing?

'Ummmmm…' Jingles began, but drifted off.

Clara managed to control herself just enough to speak. 'You. Cannot. Finish the lists. Until. Christmas Eve. That. Is. The. Point!'

'Actually,' Cocoa chipped in, 'our efficiency rate will be much higher if we know, in advance, which child is in which box. So now we do.' Cocoa looked at Clara as if she were stupid.

'Oh, really?' Clara felt her left eye twitching rapidly.

'Statistics show—' Nick started to explain.

'Stop!' Clara was almost shouting now. She lowered her voice. 'Please. Stop.'

'But productivity levels—' Nick tried again.

'Nope!' Clara yelled. 'Nope, nope, nope, nope, nope, nope, nope!'

'But—' (*Nick couldn't understand it. Why was Clara so upset? He'd worked really hard to get everything finished. She should be thrilled.*)

'Stop!' Clara's eyes glinted with fury, her hands braced on her hips, her legs apart. Her face was as red as Mrs Claus's after baking all day, and her hair looked similar to Santa's when he'd got stuck up the chimney that time. 'You can't do that. You cannot have no one in the Undecided pile!' she shrieked, her temper steaming like a Christmas pudding on the boil. Clara heard a bird squawk outside, fleeing from her fury. She didn't care.

She pulled Nick's arm and yanked him downstairs to the workshop, Cocoa following behind.

'You broke Christmas,' Clara said, pointing to the Joy-o-Meter.

Cocoa gasped. 'The machines!'

Clara nodded sadly and closed her eyes. A tear slid slowly down her face. The Joy-o-Meter had never reached zero before, the machines had never stopped working before, and the reindeer had never stopped flying before. Clara had one last idea. She climbed on top of the counter nearest to the Joy-o-Meter and tried to push the arrow back up. But it wouldn't budge. Of course it wouldn't. It was over. Christmas was over. How was she going to tell her dad? Worse, her mum? Mary Claus had always told them they could do anything they wanted as long as they believed in themselves and worked hard. How disappointed would she be to find out that her children had failed? How disappointed would every child around the world feel on Christmas morning? Would they think they'd not been good enough for a present?

Clara couldn't stop her tears from falling. Jingles walked over to her, pausing before putting his hand on her shoulder, but Clara couldn't look at him.

'I don't understand,' said Nick, his face like a puppy's that'd been told off for chewing presents under the tree.

'We were just,' began Cocoa. 'I mean, statistically...'

Clara glared at her. 'Christmas is not about statistics.' Her voice shook as she spoke. 'It's not about logistics and it is definitely not about efficiency. You...' Clara closed her eyes again, unable to continue.

Cocoa sniffed softly as the enormity of their actions hit her.

But Nick wasn't ready to admit defeat. 'So we finished the lists, so what? That's what we

were supposed to do. I don't see how it's our fault that the Joy-o-Meter's on empty. But if you think that's the problem, why don't we just redo the boxes?'

It was worth a try, thought Clara. The four of them tipped the papers out of the Naughty boxes and began to quickly re-sort them, shoving names in all of the boxes this time. It was like a paper explosion in Santa's office. There were piles of paper under desks, between Christmas cards, and resting on mugs of hot chocolate getting steadily colder because they were too busy to drink them.

It was late afternoon by the time they were done. Clara raced down to the workshop, her heart pounding. Tears sprang to her eyes when she looked at the Joy-o-Meter. The arrow hadn't moved and the machines were still silent.

She ran back upstairs and tried tipping all the paper into the Nice box to see if that made a difference. But no, of course it didn't. Nothing did. Clara trudged outside to take the reindeer some reindeer-nog and a few candy canes for a treat, but they were all so miserable about not being able to fly, they couldn't eat – not even Flea.

They were sunk, Clara thought. Christmas was cancelled. Game over. The end.

Chapter Nine

Days to Christmas Eve: 2
Joy-o-Meter level: 0
Number of ideas to save Christmas: 0

If you're looking at how many pages are left in this book, you'll know that the story doesn't end there. But for Clara that was what it felt like. There was no hope.

News trickled down to all the elves that Christmas was cancelled. Those left making the toys by hand downed tools and went home, and the reindeer stopped training. There was no point. The mood was bleak.

Nick spent the next few hours in Santa's office, frowning at the boxes on the floor. Cocoa packed the toys away in the stockroom. Jingles made hot chocolate for everyone, then joined Twinkle-Toes and Candy Cane in consoling the reindeer and bedding them down for the night. Clara was grateful – she wasn't sure she could face her furry friends after her humongous failure.

Clara walked around Santa's office and noticed the map on the wall with pins marking all the places he would have visited. She sighed. Clara knew that if she felt miserable, her reindeer must too, and she suddenly wanted to comfort them before she told her parents how much she and Nick had messed things up. Clara trundled out into the snow, thinking about the past five days and the two weeks before that. It had been relentless – with the wild reindeer getting sick and then the flying reindeer. Everything had seemed sunk then. But the reindeer had started recovering and suddenly hope and then excitement had crackled in the air. Because everyone had believed. Believed that Christmas would happen, believed that the magic of the season would make it happen, and believed in themselves because hope was there.

Clara stopped. That was it! She turned around and raced back to the workshop. She had to get Nick. He was the key! And the boxes on the floor. That was when it'd all started to go really wrong. When hope had been taken away.

Clara rushed into Santa's office, her cheeks flushed from excitement and the cold. She headed straight towards Dad's cabinet and started pulling open drawers, yanking out folders and cards and papers and even more lists.

'Clara!' Nick stared at the carnage she'd created on the floor.

'It's in here somewhere,' she replied breathlessly. Clara slammed one drawer shut and tugged open another. She gasped. She'd found it.

Clara gracefully scooped her arm into the drawer and pulled out an object covered in a faded yellow cloth. Carefully, she unwrapped it and revealed a glistening glass globe. Inside was a replica of the North Pole forest with the frozen lake and the magic crystal cave at the very centre. The

rest of the globe was filled with sparkling snow. She looked intensely into the globe lying on her upturned palm and whispered, 'Show me hope.'

Nick frowned. 'The Snow Globe?' he asked. 'I thought it was only for emergencies.'

Clara smiled and kept her eyes on the globe. This was an emergency. She had to show Nick hope. He had to understand what had happened when he'd taken it away from all those children.

'Show me,' whispered Clara again. 'Please.'

The lights in Santa's office dimmed. The snow inside the ball swirled like a blizzard. The Snow Globe grew brighter, now the only source of light in the room. Gradually the snow inside it slowed, twinkling like lights on a tree. It started settling slowly, drifting softly to the floor, and an image appeared in the lake.

It showed a room, painted blue, a stencil of a red boat on one wall. A child lay in a rumpled bed, head under the covers, sobbing silently. The door opened and a girl tiptoed in wearing pyjamas, her hair ruffled, her eyes bleary.

'Hey,' she whispered, 'budge up.'

The covers were pulled back. A boy of about six looked up at her. His eyes were wet and wide; his bottom lip trembled. He scootched to one side as the girl climbed into bed and cuddled him.

'I had… a… b-b-b-bad… dream,' he whimpered.

'Shhh,' she soothed. 'I'm here now.' And she cradled her brother tight and sung softly, lulling him to sleep.

The picture blurred and once more the globe was filled with snow. The office lights flickered and began to shine brightly again.

A slip of paper floated from the ceiling, like a feather, landing in front of Nick. He read it out loud: 'Aisha was on the Naughty list three days before Christmas. When their mum was asleep, recovering from flu, Aisha wanted her to rest, so she comforted her younger brother who was having a bad dream. She went straight to the Nice list.'

Clara looked at her brother. Nick just shrugged.

'She probably wanted to go to sleep herself but couldn't because of the crying. She was on the Naughty list for a reason, Clara.'

Before Clara could answer him, the lights flickered and dimmed once more, and the Snow Globe swirled into action.

Now it showed a classroom. A boy a few years younger than Clara stood near the snack bowl, eyes darting around the room. When he thought no one was looking, he grabbed a packet of raisins and devoured them. The scene jumped ahead, showing a girl bursting into tears.

'What's the matter, Hannah?' asked the teacher.

Through sobs, Hannah answered, 'There… are… no… more raisins… left.'

The teacher looked around the room, frowning. 'Has someone had two snacks again? There was enough for everybody.'

The scene jumped once more and a kitchen

appeared. A man and woman were whispering furiously, their heads together. The boy from the classroom watched them, hidden in the doorway.

'I'm fine,' whispered the woman. 'I don't need dinner.'

'You're working tonight. You need to eat something,' insisted the man.

The woman shook her head. 'You need it,' she said.

The boy strolled into the room. 'Can I have a snack instead of dinner?' he asked. 'I'm still full from lunch at school.'

'Are you sure, Connor?' his mum asked.

'Uh, yeah,' he replied, as if it was a stupid question. Both parents smiled, looking relieved as they dished up two small plates of dinner

for themselves. The scene flashed, jumping to Connor in his room eating a packet of raisins from a stash under his bed.

Snow filled the globe again and the image disappeared.

The lights in the office flickered on and another note fluttered to the floor.

'Santa moved Connor to the Nice list after that,' Nick read from the slip of paper. He shook his head. 'Look, I get it but… he stole.'

'Raisins,' Clara pointed out. 'So that both his parents could eat dinner that night.'

'Stealing is still stealing.

The lights flickered once more and the Snow Globe swirled, its light beaming across the room. The snow settled, but this time the scene remained white.

A robin lay on the ground, motionless. A boy walked across a blanket of snow, crushing it beneath his feet as he trudged along the path. He stopped, squinted, and changed direction towards the lifeless robin. Crouching down, he looked around him, but there was no one to help. The boy swallowed as he raised his finger, which shook as he stroked the bird. It didn't move. Quickly, he unwrapped his scarf, lifted the bird and cradled it in a warm woolly cocoon.

'Let's get you some help,' he cooed and made his way back across the snow, his feet slipping on the icy ground, forcing him to slow down. 'I won't let you die alone,' he whispered to the robin.

The image blurred and the office lights beamed on again.

Clara swallowed and looked at Nick through tears that were streaking down her face. Nick looked as white as the Snow Globe and another piece of paper fell into his trembling hand.

'What happened?' Clara whispered.

'The boy had been on the Naughty List until he saved the robin last Christmas Eve,' read Nick.

'And the robin?' asked Clara.

Nick looked at her, his eyes glinting. 'The robin is currently a Santa Scout in Australia,' he finished reading.

Clara looked at her brother and waited. He pursed his lips and lowered his eyebrows.

'There has to be hope, Nick,' Clara urged. 'Without hope there's nothing.' When Nick stayed silent, Clara continued, 'If we'd known a few days ago that the machines would break down, the reindeer would stop flying, the elves would stop working, and Christmas would be cancelled, do you think we would've tried to save Christmas?'

Nick pouted. 'We might have.'

'Really? If we knew that we were going to fail, would we really have put ourselves through all of this… urgh.' Clara could not think of a word to describe her frustration so settled on a sound effect instead.

'You would have,' Nick said quietly.

Clara frowned. 'What?'

'You would have,' he repeated. 'Tried anyway.

You're doing it now. You're still trying to save Christmas.'

Clara raised one shoulder to her chin. She didn't know what to say to that.

'There has to be hope, Nick,' she repeated. 'There has to be a light – a chance for everything to be fine. A spark, a miracle, or whatever, but something. Some hope that might make everything okay. When you put all those children in the Naughty box, you took away their hope, so they stopped trying—'

'But,' interrupted Nick, 'how would they even know?'

'Because children know, Nick. They know when no one expects anything of them. They know when people stop believing in them or when they've given up. Children can feel it.

Look, not everyone is going to be amazing at everything. You're great at lists and organising, and I'm better with people and reindeer. It doesn't make me better than you, or you better than me, it just makes us different. All children deserve a chance to show what they're good at and that they are kind and caring and loving.'

Nick smiled sadly, tears glazing his eyes. 'I failed, didn't I?'

Clara put her arm around her brother's shoulders. 'You just lost your way a little,' she replied, hugging him, 'but we brought you back.'

'Like the children in the Snow Globe,' Nick realised.

'I guess so,' Clara replied, crinkling her nose. 'Don't get all mushy on me though!'

Nick moved towards the boxes and sat cross-legged on the floor. He picked up a piece of paper from the Naughty pile and began to read.

Clara looked downstairs to the dial on the wall. The Joy-o-Meter was on three.

CHAPTER TEN

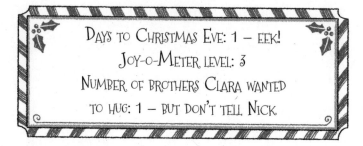

DAYS TO CHRISTMAS EVE: 1 – EEK!
JOY-O-METER LEVEL: 3
NUMBER OF BROTHERS CLARA WANTED
TO HUG: 1 – BUT DON'T TELL NICK

As they re-sorted the boxes for the second time, Clara watched Nick closely. She could tell he was taking care with each piece of paper, making sure that every child still had hope. In fact, the seventeen Naughty boxes were almost empty. Children around the world would still have a chance to show they could be nice before Christmas Eve.

When it was finally done (for now), Nick and Clara walked downstairs into Santa's Toy

Workshop. The noise of machines whirring and churning hit them. Fluff filled the air as teddy-bears were stuffed. Cocoa walked around with her clipboard, organising the elves already running into the workshop in their green overalls, ready to get back to work.

Clara smiled. Next stop, the stables.

Before they'd even rounded the corner, Clara saw something in the sky.

'Is that…?' asked Nick, running alongside Clara.

Clara nodded, tears brimming in her eyes. Nova flew over their heads, swooping down and shooting back up again. 'There's no stopping my super Nova,' laughed Clara.

Jingles was standing open-mouthed outside the stables. 'I don't understand what happened,' he said. 'She just started flying again.'

'The Joy-o-Meter's on three,' Clara replied. It was the only explanation needed.

Jingles looked at Nick. 'How?' he asked.

Nick shrugged, but couldn't look Jingles in the eye. (*He couldn't believe he'd nearly ruined everything. He'd wanted to prove he could be just like his dad, but instead he'd almost sunk Christmas!*)

Clara bumped Nick's hip with her bottom, trying to ease his embarrassment. 'Nick found his Christmas Spirit,' she said, beaming.

Jingles clapped him on the back.

'Are the rest of the reindeer flying too?' Nick checked.

Jingles nodded. 'Dasher is quicker than ever!'

'I bet Lickety's thrilled,' snorted Clara.

Jingles chuckled. 'When Dasher lapped him this morning, he was so cross that he stomped into the stables and trampled straight into a bucket. You should have seen him, Clara! He was clanging about with this metal thing stuck on his hoof!'

Clara and Nick giggled with Jingles, and the North Pole filled with the sound of laughter.

🍬 🍬 🍬

It was well past their bedtime, but Clara and Nick still had so much to do. There was only twenty-four hours until Christmas Eve, so they went back to Santa's office to consult Nick's to-do list. For the first time ever, Clara was grateful for Nick's efficiency.

Messages were coming in thick and fast from the Santa Scouts by phone, email, and winged post, with birds flying in and out of the office.

'Okay, thanks,' Nick said as he ended a call. He paused, frowning.

'You all right, Nick?' Clara asked.

'Yeah, I…' Nick pursed his lips. 'It's bad behaviour but they are trying, so…' Nick put a name into the Nearly Nice box. He had started to see the good in everybody and the more he believed in them, the more they believed in themselves. Hope had returned, bringing stockings full of Christmas Spirit back to the North Pole. Nick had even started singing, and Clara had decided not to say anything about him being completely out of tune. They began to make new Naughty and Nice lists and Clara checked every name. Twice.

They worked all night and all the next day to get the last jobs done. Cocoa organised the toy quotas, Clara went through the last bits of reindeer training, Jingles checked the sleigh routes, and Nick dealt with last-minute changes to the Naughty and Nice lists, whilst keeping a close eye on the Joy-o-Meter. He didn't want it to drop again! Would they get everything done in time? Every elf, child, and reindeer worked with very little rest in between. Clara knew she wouldn't be able to sleep, even if she wanted to (which she didn't!).

Finally, the clock struck midnight. It was officially Christmas Eve.

Clara looked at her watch and bubbles fizzed inside her. Her heart was pa-rum-pum-pum-puming. Christmas crackers! There was no time left.

She and Nick were loading sacks onto the sleigh. This had to be done in a specific way, which thankfully Nick had in hand. Everything had to be in reverse order of deliveries. Hawaii (the last stop on Santa's route) had their presents packed first and New Zealand's (Santa's first stop) were packed last. This meant that all the presents were in the right place for the right time.

'I've been thinking,' Nick said as he hefted the last sack on board. 'I'm the oldest, so driving the sleigh should be my job.'

Clara felt her bubbles begin to burst.

'But…' Nick continued.

Clara held her breath.

'Merry Christmas, Clara,' he whispered, gesturing to the driver's seat.

Clara squealed and flung herself at her brother. This. Was. Going. To. Be. Awesome!

Chapter Eleven

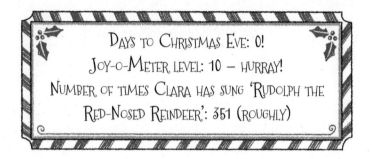

Days to Christmas Eve: 0!
Joy-o-Meter level: 10 – hurray!
Number of times Clara has sung 'Rudolph the
Red-Nosed Reindeer': 351 (roughly)

'Ho! Ho! Ho!'

Clara swung around at the booming voice. 'Dad!'

'Couldn't miss the big day, could I?' bellowed Santa.

He opened his arms and Clara ran in for a hug (her dad gave the best hugs, all snuggly and smooshy). She felt him kiss the top of her head.

'I'm so proud of you both,' Santa whispered as he embraced Nick too. Clara glowed. If her outsides could show how her insides felt, a flaming beam would be shining across the North Pole, illuminating the sky brighter than the Northern Lights.

'Hey, save some of those hugs for me,' Mary Claus called, grinning as she shuffled towards them in her slippers. As soon as her mum reached them, Clara was covered in kisses. 'Dr Elfman has given us a clean bill of health!'

'Complete rest, just as I prescribed.' Dr Elfman nodded smugly. 'It worked wonders.'

'We are all better, my gorgeous pair,' continued Mrs Claus. 'Thank you both for doing such an amazing job.'

Clara brushed away unexpected tears. If her parents knew the truth, they wouldn't think that, Clara was sure of it.

'You never gave up,' boomed Santa.

Nick and Clara frowned at their dad. How did he know?

Santa tapped a finger to his nose. 'Scouts everywhere,' he chortled.

Of course, thought Clara, rolling her eyes. Spiders, moths, birds. They were all reporting back to Santa. He really did know everything.

Clara smiled as Binky hugged Cocoa and then checked her clipboard. Like father like daughter!

Elves gathered around as Clara buckled the reindeer into their reins and did a last check of the sleigh. Everything is as it should be, thought Clara as she pushed away her disappointment that she wouldn't be on the sleigh tonight after all, now Santa was back. Clara looked at Nick. They'd done it. They'd actually saved Christmas. Nick smiled back at her.

Clara and Nick stood next to their dad by the sleigh as he did his Christmas Eve speech.

'I want to thank each and every one of you for working so hard this Christmas. It's not been easy, especially because I've not had any Christmas cookies yet. Ho! Ho! Ho!'

The elves chuckled.

'And special thanks to Nick and Clara,' Santa added, turning to look at them. 'You've made me and your mum very happy.'

Clara felt her cheeks heat up.

'Good job, sis,' said Nick as Santa continued his speech. 'I think you saved Christmas all on your own.'

Clara smiled. 'Not without your Christmas spinner.'

'Toy Popularity Prediction Algorithm,' groaned Nick.

'I know,' Clara said with a wink.

Nick shook his head and laughed. (*It was typical of Clara,*

*he thought, to still be winding him up — even
on Christmas Eve.*)

'Come on, you two,' grumbled Santa with
a grin. 'We haven't got all night, you know!'

Mum nudged Clara from behind and nodded
at the sleigh. 'Have fun!'

They didn't mean? *Oh, jingle bells!* Clara
pointed to herself. 'Me? I'm coming with you?
To deliver presents?'

Her mum and dad nodded.

'Of course, Clara Claus — you, and Nick too,'
boomed Santa. 'It seems only fair, since it was
you who rescued Christmas.'

'Woo hoo!' hollered Clara, running to the
sleigh and leaping in. 'Merry Christmas, Dad.'

'Merry Christmas, Clara. Merry Christmas, Nick.'

Nick jumped in, and with a 'Ho! Ho! Ho!

And away we go!' off they flew. Wind blew into Clara's face and she laughed at the thrill. Her stomach lurched as the sleigh swooped up and down in the sky, circling back to wave goodbye to the elves and Mrs Claus below. Dr Elfman was still at her side, pestering her to go indoors

to avoid catching a cold. Mum shrugged him off and waved and clapped with everyone else.

Clara's hair whipped around her face as the cold air kissed her skin. She was so happy she thought she might pop. Around her was the most incredible sight she'd ever seen. Thousands of stars were twinkling, sparkling like tiny gems. The tips of the forest trees were covered in gleaming snow, exactly like the Snow Globe, Clara realised with a smile. Ahead she could see land that seemed lit up with millions of fairy lights. When they got closer, Clara realised they were street lamps and lights from cars, something she'd never seen before. Beside her, Nick made notes and Clara couldn't blame him. This was nothing like the North Pole.

'Whoa!' yelped Clara as they approached their first stop – a tall, thin building that illuminated the sky in changing colours.

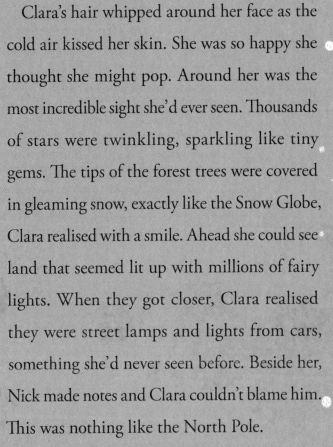

Nick flicked to a page in his notebook. 'It's the Sky Tower in New Zealand,' he proudly announced.

Clara had never heard of it, but it certainly towered up in the sky. She grinned. Soon, the children of New Zealand would be receiving their presents – and not long after, the rest of the world too. She'd done it. (With a little help from Nick. And Jingles. And Cocoa. Candy Cane. Mistletoe. Okay, all the elves. And the reindeer.) Yes, Clara Claus had saved Christmas, and thank Christmas stockings for that.

THE END

TURN THE PAGE FOR MORE FESTIVE FUN FROM CLARA, NICK AND THE ELVES!

Clara's special version of Jingle bells

Jingle bells, jingle bells,
Jingle all the way.
Oh what fun it is to ride
On a reindeer every day.

Jingle bells, jingle bells,
Jingle all the way;
Oh what fun it is to ride
In Santa's bright red sleigh.

Dashing through the snow
My Dad will guide the sleigh
O'er the fields we'll go
Ho Ho-ing all the way.

All the elves will sing
Making spirits bright
We'll stand together carolling
Oh what a special night!

Clara's Christmas List

Thermal gloves
(for reindeer training)

Thermal socks
(see above)

Red scarf
(current scarf is starting to fray)

New Book
(for bedtime)

Hot chocolate mug
(a nice big one to fit
more hot chocolate in!)

Nick's Christmas List

Notebook
(must have lines)

Pen
(black not blue)

Stopwatch
(to help with the schedules)

Jumper
(with a picture of dad on)

Book
(preferably of maps)

Here's a blank list so you can write your own.
Remember it's the thought that counts so Santa
Claus may choose to get you something instead.

My Christmas List

Dear Santa (Clara, Nick and Mrs Claus)

_____

_____

_____

_____

_____

_____

_____

_____

_____

_____

```
R  O  C  K  E  T  A  B  C  P  H
C  U  P  I  D  D  E  F  G  R  A
L  C  D  H  I  O  A  J  I  A  L
I  O  A  O  K  E  N  L  R  N  L
C  O  N  M  L  N  Y  N  R  C  E
K  K  C  F  O  P  P  E  E  E  V
E  I  E  O  P  N  H  X  M  R  E
T  E  R  I  M  S  O  I  Q  R  S
Y  S  Z  T  A  E  U  V  V  W  P
X  Y  Z  D  A  B  T  C  A  D  A
B  L  I  T  Z  E  N  E  F  G  H
```

Can you find all of Clara's reindeer in the grid above?

Blitzen	Dasher	Prancer
Comet	Donner	Rocket
Cookie	Flea	Rudolph
Cupid	Halle	Vespa
Merri	Lickety	Vixen
Dancer	Nova	Zippy

Paper Christmas Trees

These beautiful trees are simple to make. Clara likes to make these with the younger elves as it's something that everyone can do together. Remember; be careful with the scissors and the stapler (you may need a grown up to help you).

You will need:

- A4 Green craft paper or card
- Craft paper or card in other colours
- Sticky tape or stapler
- PVA glue
- String or ribbon (*optional*)

Method:

Job one Take the green card and cut it in half. Then cut it in half again so it is now a quarter of the size. You should now have four rectangles.

Job two Fold the card lengthways accordion style (like you are making a fan).

Job three Fasten one end of the paper, at the very tip, with either a stapler or sticky tape. The green paper should now look like a Christmas tree,

Job four the tree needs decorations. Using the coloured card, cut out small circles and stick them on the tree with PVA glue. Don't forget a star for the top of the tree!

Job five (*optional*) if you want to hang the tree on your own tree, thread wrapping ribbon, string or cotton through the top of the tree.

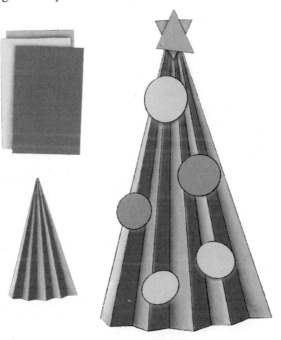

Clara's Chocolate Chip Cookies

Ingredients

- **120g** butter, softened
- **75g** light brown sugar
- **75g** caster sugar
- **1** egg
- **1** tsp vanilla extract
- **180g** plain flour
- **½ tsp** bicarbonate of soda
- **¼ tsp** salt
- **165g** chocolate chunks

  (*Clara likes to use chunks which she breaks up from a bar of chocolate*)

Method

1. Pre-heat the oven to **180c/160c fan oven/gas mark 4**. Get a grown up to help you with this and remember ovens are hot!

2. Line two baking trays with greaseproof paper or parchment paper.

3. Cream the butter, the caster sugar and the light brown sugar together in a bowl until the mixture is fluffy and pale.

4. Beat in the egg and the vanilla extract and mix well.

5. Stir in the flour, bicarbonate of soda, the salt and the chocolate.

6. Scoop large tablespoons of the mixture onto the lined baking trays. Remember to leave enough space for the cookies to spread!

7. **Bake for 10-12 minutes** or until the cookies are firm at the edges and soft in the middle (they will harden as they cool). Make sure a grown up helps you remove the cookies from the oven!

8. Leave to cool for a few moments before carefully transferring to a cooling tray.

9. Enjoy delicious chocolate chip cookie yumminess!

ACKNOWLEDGEMENTS

Clara Claus has a very special place in my heart and there are some very special people I'd like to thank for getting her out into the world. To Helen Boyle who believed from the very beginning and much like Clara never gave up. Thank you for seeing Clara's magic and for reminding me to believe in myself. To Catherine Coe who made Clara even more sparkly and special. To James Shaw and the team at Tiny Tree for providing Clara with such a welcoming home. To Louise Forshaw whose illustrations are phenomenal and capture Clara perfectly. To Mark who puts up with my endless lists, my Christmas obsession and for liking Christmas songs as much as I do. Thank you for reading first drafts and my final drafts (and all the drafts in between), I would be lost without you. To my Dad, I miss you. To Daisy who is my source of eternal joy. To my mum who always taught me that little drops make big rivers, this one is for you. Je t'aime Maman. To my friends and family who have encouraged me and supported me, you are all fantastic.

Finally I would like to thank all the readers and children out there. May you always believe in yourself and each other.

About the Author

Bonnie's all-time favourite season is Christmas, so it came as no surprise that she has written a story about it. She is her happiest in a land of imagination and the more Christmas magic and festive fun, the better. Having worked as an actress for nearly a decade Bonnie has performed in many a Christmas show. She has portrayed a rather pink and sparkly fairy bow-belles and has even dressed as a Christmas present (don't ask).

Bonnie lives in Hampshire with her husband and daughter. When she's not writing, or hunting down Christmas decorations, Bonnie works as a Learning Support Assistant at an infant school which is the perfect age to test her stories out on.

www.bonniebridgmanauthor.wixsite.com/bonnieb

Facebook: BonnieBridgman:Author

Twitter: @BonnieMrsbbh

Instagram: bonniebridgmanauthor